Sophia

It's Time to Sleep, My Love

ILLUSTRATED BY

Nancy Tillman

WRITTEN BY Eric Metaxas

NEW YORK

"It's time to sleep, it's time to sleep,"
the fishes croon in waters deep.

It's time to sleep   It's time to sleep

The songbirds sing in trees above,
"It's time to sleep, my love, my love."

"It's time to sleep, my love."

"So, go to sleep, my sleepy child,"
the tiger whispers in the wild.

The otter utters by the lake,
"It's getting hard to stay awake."

"So, go to sleep, my love."

"Let's go to sleep, my darling love,"
so coos the sleepy turtledove.

So drones the drowsy bumblebee
inside its hive inside its tree,

"Let's go to sleep, my love."

"I'm getting very sleepy now,"
so moos the tired milking cow.

I'm getting very
sleepy now

So croaks the almost-sleeping frog
amidst the settling of the fog,

I'm getting very sleepy now

"So, go to sleep, my love."

Your dreams will be arriving soon.
They'll float to you
in sleep's balloon.

They'll be here when I snuff the wick,
you'd better close your eyelids quick.
So you can dream, my love, my love.
So you can dream, my love.

And as you dream inside your sleep,
the fishes crooning in the deep, and
all the songbirds up above
will sleep and dream of you, my love,
of you, the one I love.

It's time to sleep

To Mama, who shared her lap and her love of books with me before I could walk,
and to my wonderful husband, Rick, my biggest cheerleader.
—N.T.

To them, the ones we love.
—E.M.

A FEIWEL AND FRIENDS BOOK
An Imprint of Macmillan

Library of Congress Cataloging-in-Publication Data Available

ISBN-13: 978-0-312-38371-8
ISBN-10: 0-312-38371-1

The artwork is created digitally using a variety of software painting programs, on a Wacom tablet. Layers of illustrative elements are first individually created,
then merged to form a composite. At this point, texture and mixed media (primarily chalk, watercolor, and pencil) are applied to complete each illustration.

Feiwel and Friends logo designed by Filomena Tuosto

First Edition: October 2008

10 9 8 7 6 5 4 3 2 1

www.feiwelandfriends.com

You are loved.